W9-AXY-808

WITHDRAWN

THE STORMY ADVENTURE OF ABBIE BURGESS,

LIGHTHOUSE KEEPER

BY **PETER ROOP** AND **CONNIE ROOP**
ADAPTATION BY **AMANDA DOERING TOURVILLE**
ILLUSTRATED BY **ZACHARY TROVER**

Graphic Universe™ Minneapolis • New York

INTRODUCTION

FOR CENTURIES, LIGHTHOUSES HAVE WARNED SAILORS OF DANGER ALONG COASTS. MOST MODERN LIGHTHOUSES USE MACHINES, INSTEAD OF PEOPLE, TO KEEP THE LIGHTS LIT. THEY ALSO HAVE ELECTRICITY, RADAR, AND RADIO TO AID THEM IN THEIR IMPORTANT JOBS. BUT LONG AGO, SIMPLE LAMPS AND DEDICATED LIGHTHOUSE KEEPERS WERE ALL THAT KEPT MANY SHIPS FROM BEING WRECKED ON DANGEROUS ROCKS AND LEDGES.

IN 1853, ABBIE BURGESS AND HER FAMILY MOVED TO MATINICUS ROCK, OFF THE COAST OF MAINE. ABBIE'S FATHER BECAME THE LIGHTHOUSE KEEPER THERE. THE FAMILY HAD TO KEEP THE LIGHTS BURNING NO MATTER WHAT—OR SHIPS WOULD SINK AND PEOPLE WOULD DIE.

MATINICUS ROCK, MAINE
JANUARY 16, 1856
EARLY EVENING

CAN YOU SEE THE LIGHTHOUSE? THE COAST IS HERE SOMEWHERE.

5

THE DAY PASSED QUICKLY.

THE WIND AND RAIN CONTINUED TO POUND MATINICUS ROCK. AGAIN THAT NIGHT, ABBIE LIT THE LAMPS IN BOTH LIGHTHOUSE TOWERS.

THESE TOWERS ARE BUILT TO WITHSTAND STORMS. WE'LL BE SAFER IN HERE.

THE STORM BUILT FOR DAYS. FOR A WHILE, THE FAMILY HAD TO MOVE INTO ONE OF THE LIGHTHOUSE TOWERS.

THE WAVES WASHED AWAY
THE HENHOUSE, BUT THE
LIGHTHOUSE AND STONE
BUILDINGS STILL STOOD.

THE STORM RAGED ON FOR WEEKS.
FOOD WAS RUNNING OUT.

IT'S A GOOD THI
I WAS ABLE TO S
THOSE CHICKENS

ALL WE HAVE TO
EAT ARE EGGS AND
DRIED FRUIT.

BLECH! I'M SO
SICK OF EGGS!

AFTERWORD

ABBIE BURGESS CONTINUED TO TAKE CARE OF LIGHTHOUSES FOR THE
REST OF HER LIFE. SHE HELPED TRAIN HER FATHER'S SUCCESSOR,
CAPTAIN JOHN GRANT, IN 1861. ABBIE SOON MARRIED HIS SON, ISAAC,
AND SHE WAS APPOINTED ASSISTANT KEEPER AT MATINICUS ROCK. THE
COUPLE HAD FOUR CHILDREN. THEY BECAME KEEPERS AT WHITEHEAD
LIGHT LIGHTHOUSE IN 1875. ABBIE DIED IN 1892. IN 1945, HER GRAVE WAS
MARKED BY A SMALL METAL LIGHTHOUSE.

IN 1997, THE U.S. COAST GUARD COMMISSIONED A SHIP IN HONOR
OF ABBIE BURGESS, THE BRAVE LIGHTHOUSE KEEPER. THE USCGC
ABBIE BURGESS IS DOCKED IN ROCKLAND, MAINE. THE SHIP SERVICES
THE MAINE COAST AND THE SAINT CROIX RIVER. THE SHIP'S CREW IS
RESPONSIBLE FOR LIGHTING FLOATING AIDS THAT ALERT OTHER SHIPS
OF UNSAFE AREAS.

FURTHER READING AND WEBSITES

GLEASON, CARRIE. *OCEAN STORM ALERT!* NEW YORK: CRABTREE PUBLISHING, 2005.

HOUSE, KATHERINE L. *LIGHTHOUSES FOR KIDS: HISTORY, SCIENCE, AND LORE WITH 21 ACTIVITIES.* CHICAGO: CHICAGO REVIEW PRESS, 2008.

LEGENDARY LIGHTHOUSES
HTTP://WWW.PBS.ORG/LEGENDARYLIGHTHOUSES/

THE LIGHTHOUSE DIRECTORY
HTTP://WWW.UNC.EDU/~ROWLETT/LIGHTHOUSE/

MATINICUS ROCK LIGHTHOUSE HISTORY
HTTP://LIGHTHOUSE.CC/MATINICUSROCK/HISTORY.HTML

NATIONAL SEVERE STORMS LABORATORY
HTTP://WWW.NSSL.NOAA.GOV/EDU/

PLISSON, PHILLIP. *LIGHTHOUSES.* NEW YORK: ABRAMS BOOKS FOR YOUNG READERS, 2005.

SIMON, SEYMORE. *OCEANS.* NEW YORK: COLLINS, 2006.

STAINTON, SUE. *THE LIGHTHOUSE CAT.* NEW YORK: KATHERINE TEGREN BOOKS, 2004.

VAN RYNBACH, IRIS. *SAFELY TO SHORE: AMERICA'S LIGHTHOUSES.* WATERTOWN, MA: CHARLESBRIDGE, 2003.

VAUGHAN, MARCIA K. *ABBIE AGAINST THE STORM: THE TRUE STORY OF A YOUNG HEROINE AND A LIGHTHOUSE.* PORTLAND, OR: BEYOND WORDS PUBLISHING, 1999.

WOLFMAN, JUDY. *LIFE ON A CHICKEN FARM.* MINNEAPOLIS: LERNER PUBLICATIONS COMPANY, 2003.

ABOUT THE AUTHORS

PETER ROOP AND CONNIE ROOP HAVE WRITTEN MANY BOOKS FOR CHILDREN. AS LONGTIME TEACHERS, THEY VALUE THE POWER OF WELL-WRITTEN STORIES THAT CAN INSPIRE THEIR READERS WITH THE NOTION THAT ANYTHING IS POSSIBLE. WHEN NOT TRAVELING WORLDWIDE OR SHARING THEIR LOVE OF READING AND WRITING IN SCHOOLS, THE ROOPS LIVE IN WISCONSIN.

ABOUT THE ADAPTER

AMANDA DOERING TOURVILLE HAS WRITTEN MORE THAN 40 BOOKS FOR CHILDREN. AMANDA IS GREATLY HONORED TO WRITE FOR YOUNG PEOPLE AND HOPES THAT THEY WILL LEARN TO LOVE READING AND LEARNING AS MUCH AS SHE DOES. WHEN NOT WRITING, AMANDA ENJOYS TRAVELING, PHOTOGRAPHY, AND HIKING. SHE LIVES IN MINNESOTA WITH HER HUSBAND AND GUINEA PIG.

ABOUT THE ILLUSTRATOR

ZACHARY TROVER HAS BEEN DRAWING SINCE HE WAS OLD ENOUGH TO HOLD A PENCIL AND HASN'T STOPPED YET. YOU CAN FIND HIM LIVING SOMEWHERE IN THE MIDWEST WITH HIS EXTREMELY PATIENT WIFE AND TWO EXTREMELY IMPATIENT DOGS.

Text copyright © 2011 by Peter Roop and Connie Roop
Illustrations © 2011 by Lerner Publishing Group, Inc.

Graphic Universe™ is a trademark of Lerner Publishing Group, Inc.

Graphic Universe™
A division of Lerner Publishing Group, Inc.
241 First Avenue North
Minneapolis, MN 55401 U.S.A.

Website address: www.lernerbooks.com

Library of Congress Cataloging-in-Publication Data

Roop, Peter.
    The stormy adventure of Abbie Burgess, lighthouse keeper / by Peter Roop and Connie Roop ; adapted by Amanda
  Doering Tourville ; illustrated by Zachary Trover.
        p.   cm. — (History's kid heroes)
    Includes bibliographical references.
    ISBN: 978-0-7613-6172-5 (lib. bdg. : alk. paper)
        1. Burgess, Abbie, 1839-1892—Juvenile literature. 2. Lighthouse keepers—Maine—Biography—Juvenile literature.
3. Matinicus Rock Lighthouse (Matinicus Rock, Me.)—Juvenile literature. 4. Burgess, Abbie, 1839–1892—Comic books,
strips, etc. 5. Lighthouse keepers—Maine—Biography—Comic books, strips, etc. 6. Matinicus Rock Lighthouse
(Matinicus Rock, Me.)—Comic books, strips, etc. 7. Graphic novels. I. Roop, Connie. II. Tourville, Amanda Doering, 1980–
III. Trover, Zachary, ill. IV. Title.
VK1140.B87R66 2011
387.1'55092—dc22 [B]   2010006748

Manufactured in the United States of America
1—CG—7/15/10